Up and at 'Em with
Winnie & Ernst

Gina Freschet

Farrar Straus Giroux

New York

To my friend and editor, Robbie Mayes

Copyright © 2005 by Gina Freschet
All rights reserved
Distributed in Canada by Douglas & McIntyre Publishing Group
Color separations by Chroma Graphics PTE Ltd.
Printed and bound in the United States of America
by Phoenix Color Corporation
Typography by Jay Colvin
First edition, 2005
1 3 5 7 9 10 8 6 4 2

Library of Congress Cataloging-in-Publication Data
Freschet, Gina.
  Up and at 'em with Winnie & Ernst / Gina Freschet.— 1st ed.
    p. cm.
  Summary: Follows the humorous adventures of best friends Winnie
the possum and Ernst the otter as they break their piggy bank, baby-sit
eggs, hold a telescope party, and enter a poetry contest.
  ISBN-13: 0-978-0-374-38446-3
  ISBN-10: 0-374-38446-0
  [1. Best friends—Fiction. 2. Friendship—Fiction. 3. Opossums—
Fiction. 4. Otters—Fiction. 5. Animals—Fiction. 6. Humorous
stories.] I. Title: Up and at them with Winnie & Ernst. II. Title.

PZ7.F889685Up 2005
[E]—dc22

2003056375

Contents

Winnie and Ernst's Piggy Bank

Winnie and Ernst shared a piggy bank. They were saving up for a trip to Backwater Beach Amusement Park.

Chink, chink, chink! Winnie loved the sound of coins in the piggy bank. Sometimes before bed, she shook it and listened to it jingle.

Then, one day in June, the piggy bank was full. "And it's a perfect day for the beach," Winnie said as she pulled on her bathing cap.

Ernst carried the piggy bank all the way to Backwater Beach.

At last, the moment they'd been waiting for had come. "Farewell, Piggy!" sang Winnie.

Holding a tiny hammer, Ernst said, "Ready? One . . . two . . . two and a half . . . two . . . and THREE!" He smashed the piggy bank as Winnie squealed with delight.

But after searching among the pieces, she stammered, "There's hardly any coins!"

Instead, Ernst had filled the bank with other things he wanted to save.

"What are these?" Winnie demanded. "Bottle caps? Seashells? Buttons?!"

"Here's some checkers and skipping rocks, too," Ernst pointed out. "And my lucky orange peels."

"But where are all the quarters?" Winnie wailed. "We can't pay for rides with orange peels."

"This is good stuff," Ernst insisted. He put two bottle caps on his eyes and the orange peel in his mouth. "Look," he said, "this is *funny*. You can't do this with quarters."

Winnie hung her head and went into a pout. It wasn't pretty.

Across the boardwalk, Ernst spied a sign painter's shop. He went in and asked to borrow some paints and brushes.

He took them back to where Winnie sat. Ernst painted googly eyes on the bottle caps and silly teeth on the orange peels.

"Look, Winnie, look," he said, until at last Winnie had to hide a smile.

"I have an idea," Ernst told her. "We'll paint all the seashells and buttons and sell them as trinkets." He sat down and painted a seagull on his favorite skipping rock.

Watching him, Winnie brightened. "I'm going to paint all the checkers like seashells," she said, "and the seashells with beach scenes, and the buttons with squids."

Before long, Winnie and Ernst had happily painted dozens of trinkets.

They even painted the broken pieces of the piggy bank with slogans like:

YOU'LL BE TO Back to Backwater!

Soon they had attracted a crowd of tourists, and by lunchtime, Winnie was gleefully counting their new pile of coins.

Feeling lucky, she played one of the carnival games.

Winnie dunked the lobster with just one throw. What did she win?

A brand-new piggy bank!

"Just what we needed," said Ernst.

"I can't wait to start saving for next year," said Winnie. And into the new bank she dropped the one thing she had saved: Ernst's favorite skipping rock.

Winnie and Ernst's Cosmic Adventure

For months and months, Winnie saved the wrappers from Froony's Green Fruit Bars. She didn't even like fruit bars—sometimes she fed them to the ducks—but she wanted the wrappers.

If she collected one hundred wrappers, she could send away for the Shark-Tooth Earrings or the Rhinestone Muscle-Band. For five hundred wrappers she could get the Big Kahuna Mask or the Secret X-Ray Glasses. But Winnie held out for the biggest prize of all.

For one thousand wrappers she could get
the Bubble Telescope, named for Professor
Bubble himself.

At last, after a thousand days and a
thousand Froony's Green Fruit Bars, Winnie
had collected enough wrappers.

She bundled them up
and sent them off.

All her friends
waited for the arrival of
Winnie's big prize. "I'll
have a viewing," she
promised. "It will be
star-studded!"

At last, the big day and the Bubble
Telescope arrived.

Winnie and Ernst set it up right away.

Winnie cooed, "It's beautiful."

"And a perfect night for stargazing," said
Ernst. But just as he said it, the wind shifted.
A big foggy cloud drifted over Winnie's house.
And stayed there.

Winnie and Ernst peered into the telescope.
There was nothing to be seen. Nothing at all.
And the guests were about to arrive.

"Oh no!" Winnie wailed. "What will we do?"

"Stall 'em," said Ernst. He ran up to the
attic and got down a box of Christmas
decorations.

With a brave face, Winnie greeted her guests.
Everyone chattered excitedly. "I want to see
Saturn," said Wally the rabbit.

"We want to see the Milky Way," said Old
Thorny the turtle and Ing the duck.

"Yes, yes," said Winnie nervously. "You'll
all get to see your favorite stars and planets."
Then she spied Ernst, ready on the roof.

Winnie patted the telescope. "First," Winnie
told the crowd, "I'd like to show you . . ." She
thought and thought, but she couldn't come
up with a single constellation.

Luckily, Ernst worked quickly with a fishing rod and Winnie's Christmas box.

"There's Saturn!" cried Wally.

"Oooh, ahhh," everyone said.

Ernst lobbed globs of glitter, and Old Thorny saw the Milky Way. "Oooh, ahhh," everyone said.

Ernst cast out a net of Christmas tree lights.

"A meteor shower! Oooh, ahhh," everyone said.

22

But Ernst got tangled in the lines and strings and hooks.

"Shooting stars!" said Birdy.

Ernst began to slide down the shingles.

Slipping, Ernst kicked the box, and everything in it went flying.

"A blazing comet!" cried Old Thorny.

Wally yelled, "A giant asteroid! It's coming right at us!"

"Run, everybody!" screamed Ing.

25

In a panic, they all ran into each other and fell into a pile.

Looking up, they saw Ernst hanging from the rain gutter, dangling decorations and looking sheepish.

Before he could speak, the wind shifted, the
big foggy cloud blew away, and everyone got
to look at their favorite planets and stars for
real.

"Oooh! Ahhh!" everyone said.

Winnie and Ernst
Go Baby-sitting

Ernst had to go baby-sitting. He got Winnie to go along by bringing lots of toys and saying, "Come on, it will be fun."

When they got to the house, Mrs. H. Penny was all ready. "I won't be long," she promised. "The children are inside. They won't be any trouble. Just be sure to keep them warm." And with that, Mrs. H. Penny flew the coop.

Inside, Winnie and Ernst saw a nest. "Oh, great," griped Winnie. "You didn't tell me they haven't even *hatched* yet!"

"Who knew?" replied Ernst.

"There's one thing *I* know," Winnie told him. "There's no way I'm sitting on that nest."

"Well, *I'm* not sitting on it."

"We have to keep them warm," Winnie insisted.

Ernst pulled pillows and blankets from the bedroom. He piled them carefully on the nest, tucking the eggs in.

"That's not warm enough," said Winnie. "Should I turn on the oven?"

"What for?" Ernst asked. "Do you want to *fry* them?"

"Well," said Winnie, "you'd better sit on top."

Reluctantly Ernst agreed.

But once he was up there, he couldn't very well leave. A dusty pillow made him sneeze. He asked, "Winnie, may I have a tissue?"

Winnie brought him a tissue.

"It's dry up here. May I have some juice?"

Winnie brought Ernst a glass of juice.

Ernst spilled some. "Winnie, would you bring me a napkin?"

She did.

Ernst sneezed again and asked, "Winnie, could you shut the window?"

Winnie shut the window.

"And I need another tissue."

Huffing, she got him one.

"May I have a magazine?"

"Of *course*." Winnie brought Ernst a magazine. Then she settled down to read one of her own.

"Winnie?" said Ernst.

"What?! What is it now?! Shine your buttons? Wipe your nose? Comb your tail?"

"Shhh," said Ernst. "Do you hear something?"

They listened. They heard a tiny *chip*.

"What was that?" said Winnie.

There was another little *chip*.

"OH NO!" they yelped. Quickly they uncovered the nest. And there were all the eggs just ready to hatch all at once.

Crack. A chick stuck its fuzzy head out. Then another, and another. With wobbly heads, the chicks looked up at Winnie. "Mommy," said one.

"Not me," said Winnie.

The hatchlings turned to Ernst. "Mommy?"

"No way," said Ernst. He and Winnie backed away as the chicks started to fluff and flap and tweak their feathers with their tiny newborn beaks.

They were hopping out of the nest faster than Winnie and Ernst could catch them and put them back in. Chasing the chicks, Ernst shouted, "It's like a popcorn popper run amok!"

At that, the front door opened, and there stood Mrs. H. Penny, all puffed up.

"My dears!" she exclaimed, and all the chicks ran to her, cheeping.

"Mommy!" they said.

Mrs. H. Penny folded them under her pillowy wings.

"Well," stammered Winnie and Ernst. "Nice seeing you. Congratulations. No charge. Gotta run."

And run they did.

Winnie and Ernst's
Poetry Contest

It was February. There was nothing to do.

Winnie had a bright idea. "I know! We'll have a poetry contest." Ernst munched on his sandwich as Winnie continued. "Everyone can compose a poem, and we'll give a prize for the best one."

"I already have a poem," said Ernst. He recited it:

"This is my poem;
 I wrote it at home."

Winnie waited. "That's it?" she said. "That's your poem?"

Ernst nodded.

Winnie put him to work. They had to make flyers to advertise. First prize for the best poem would be front-row tickets for the Spring Peeper Chorus. It wasn't easy to get good seats at the bog.

The contest was held at Town Hall. There
was quite a turnout. The poets each took a
number and waited for their name to be called.

Mrs. Buttress Badger was first up. Very pleased with herself, she recited:

"Spring
makes me sing
with the bluebells
that ring

and the breeze
that will bring
a zing
of a fling
to each wild thing."

Everyone clapped politely, but no one understood a word of it.

Next up was Webber. He croaked:

"That sinking feeling
   when the fisherman's reeling
   and the next thing you know
   you're caught by the toe . . ."

He became so emotional, he couldn't go on.
Although everybody clapped, no one
understood Webber's poem, either.

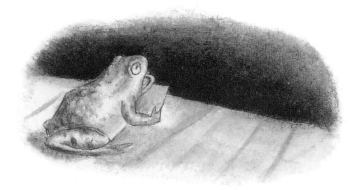

Now it was Winnie's turn. She took the
stage, smoothed her dress, cleared her throat,
and recited:

"Yesterday,
just dust in the
curtains.
Today, the mirror
is full of blue clouds."

She primly sat down. Hardly anyone
clapped, they were so confused.

But there was no mistaking the mouse's
meaning when he got up and read his poem:

"When I saw the cat
I spit and I spat.

I may be just a mouse,
but the cat is a rat
and a louse."

A cat in the audience hissed and pounced,
just missing the mouse. A rat was mad, too.
There was sniping and swiping and running
around.

Winnie and Ernst tried to break up the
fight. Then a fox leered at Wally, and a shrew
started shrieking.

"Stop it!" cried Winnie and Ernst as they
held back the angry poets. With some snarling
and squeaking, everyone stamped off in a huff.

Winnie and Ernst looked at the mess.

Ernst said, "I have another poem." And he recited it:

"Roses are red,
  violets are blue,
  since nobody won
  we've got tickets for two!"